CREATURE LOVING VOLUME 2
Lilith Leana

Table of Contents

Acknowledgement

A big thank you to my husband for always believing in me and never making me feel like I couldn't do it.

Cover art

Cover art from Depositphoto

Cover design

Lilith Leana with Canva

Brief Summary

Bathing with the Akkorokamui

Ava's trip to Japan ends in the beautiful village, Kurokawa Onsen, famous for its hot springs. She gets the most pleasurable and relaxing surprise when she enters the lair of the Akkorokamui.

Akkorokamui lives to heal people with the use of its tentacles. Ava has tension everywhere in her body, and it will do its utmost best to let her unwind in the most satisfying way possible.

Courted by El Sombrerón

Ariana went to Guatemala for her vacation, thinking she will return exactly the same. She hadn't counted on the mysterious El Sombrerón seducing her and making her his bride.

El Sombrerón has lived a lonely life, always searching for a bride, but never finding one. When the beautiful Ariana gifts him with her smile, he knows he will not rest until he has made her his bride.

Saved by the Yeti

Evelyn thinks her life is over when she gets trapped in the snow on her company ski trip. She gets saved by a massive white creature, and the moment she wakes up, the only thing she can think about is thanking her rescuer any way she can.

Jens the Yeti saved the cute little human female, trying to do the right thing. When she wakes up and rubs herself all over him, he can't resist his urge to breed her.

Mated to a Vampire

Luna Cassidy finds a Vampire in her territory who smells absolutely delectable. Her Wolf thinks he is her mate, but she doesn't want to give in to her urges before she knows why he crossed into her territory.

Elijah has to get to his Vampire Queen fast, but gets trapped in Wolf territory. When the sexy Luna tells him he is her mate, he scoffs and runs away, but something inside of him makes him turn back.

Seducing the Orc

Mia loves playing Dungeons and Dragons. Playing with a new group, she meets a shy, nerdy Orc with whom she has an instant connection. She thinks he is her Mate, now she only has to seduce him to convince him they are perfect for each other.

Gunnar has always been happy in his little bubble, playing games and not having to worry about anything else. But that changes when the gorgeous little human in his Dungeons and Dragons group states she is his Mate. She is so tiny he is afraid he will hurt her, but she is sure that they will fit together.

On a Date with the Naga

After Avery lets a Naga fuck her at her work she takes him out on a Date to get their stories straight before she loses her job.

Ezra has other plans for his date with Avery. He invites her to his appartement to double stuff her.

READER ADVISORY: THIS story contains explicit sex scenes.

Creature Loving Volume 2 is a collection of five previously published standalone short erotic stories and one exciting new bonus story.

It is filled with human FMC's loving Monsters, Beasts and Creatures. Full-length, explicit sex scenes, standalone, no cheating or cliffhangers.

Bathing with the Akkorokamui

I needed to relax. This was my first vacation in years and I would do everything in my power to relax. But I never imagined it turning out like this, wrapped up in tentacles pleasuring me like I have never experienced before.

Japan truly was a beautiful country. I had traveled all over in the past month and I had just arrived at my last destination, Kurokawa Onsen, the gorgeous village famous for its hot springs.

After a brief conversation with Aoi, the host of my Ryokan, she outlined my route, pinpointing which four hot springs I should definitely visit and where to end.

The first one, Yamamizuki's onsen was located in a forest with a flowing mountain river. I heard the birds playing in the forest and the soft murmuring of the river water. I laid my head on one of the big boulders and let the soothing sounds of nature calm me.

The second one, Yama no Yado Shinmeikan, had a beautiful cave bath. It was the polar opposite of the first where I had enjoyed the free feeling of being outside in nature. This one was dark and broody, almost as if something could come out of the waters. I didn't stay long in that one, but it was famous for a reason, and I was happy to have seen it.

My third stop was the Ryokan Ikoi, which had a standing hot spring. I had to stand up in the water, holding onto the floating bamboo while enjoying the beautiful view. It was rumored this one could make ladies prettier when they soaked in it, but I didn't believe that kind of superstition.

Each hot spring was more beautiful than the next, and I could feel myself relaxing in the hot water while enjoying the fabulous view of the Japanese bamboo forest.

The titillation of walking around naked underneath my soft bathrobe was an added bonus. No clothes were allowed in the hot springs and so far I had always been on my own in them. I figured that Aoi had chosen these deliberately for me so I could take some time to unwind in private.

My last stop, as so indicated by my host, was named Akkorokamui. I didn't know what to expect, but she had assured me it would be my most relaxing visit yet.

And now I was in a hot spring with a Japanese sea monster.

I was enjoying the hot water on my naked body and the cool wind on my heated face when I felt something stirring the water. Looking around I saw no one, I shrugged and blamed it on my overactive imagination. Being in another country always made my fantasies run wild. The vacation had been amazing, enjoying my time alone and discovering so many new things.

The smell of the yuzu lime filled my senses as I thought back on all the new tastes and scents I had discovered. I was a definite Foody and Japan was the perfect country to sate my never-ending craving for new experiences.

It had been a taxing trip trying to see all of Japan in one month. I really deserved to relax so I could return home ready for work again. The water had done a lot already to ease my aching muscles, but what I really craved was a massage. Maybe I should ask my host if there was a massage parlor nearby so I could loosen up fully before my long flight back home.

As if to answer my prayers, I felt a soft caress on the back of my calf. Thinking I was dreaming it, I held still lost in thought about a lover's touch. When the creature noted that I didn't pull back, it touched me again. This time I was certain I wasn't imagining things. I turned around and stood face to tentacle with an enormous Sea Monster.

My mouth fell open in amazement. Never before had I seen anything quite like it, it was magnificent and grotesque at the same time. Dozen of tentacles in all shapes and sizes surrounded the massive head with two unblinking black eyes. The most striking part of it all was its color. It was ruby red, the deep vibrant color only enhanced by the dying sun reflecting in the water. It almost looked like I was in a pool filled with blood, but it was its massive body that had taken over the entire hot spring.

Don't fear, Ava.

I didn't see a mouth nor did I hear the words in the air, it spoke to me through some mental soothing voice. Strangely enough, it didn't scare me. I knew that if it wanted to kill me, it could have done so already in a blink of an eye. A strange calmness came over me. I was going to let this creature have its way with me, I would relinquish full control over my body and it was the most relaxing realization ever.

Aoi has spoken to me of your ailments. Let me relieve them.

I nodded not trusting my own voice. The host of the Ryokan I was staying in had promised me a satisfying visit, and I was going to trust her and this creature.

Close your eyes and let all your worries float away, Ava.

That sounded quite lovely so I obeyed its command. I let myself lean back, floating on the water with my eyes closed. My naked breasts peeked out of the water. My nipples tightened with a cool gush of wind.

I felt weightless in the water, enjoying the freedom of not having to think and just feel. The delicate caress returned to my leg. It lowered me into the pool so only my head remained above water. With the softest sponge I have ever experienced, it traced my toes, one by one giving them each just the right amount of attention.

It was a sign of respect to entering a space with clean feet and it was as if it wanted mine to be the cleanest possible. When it was satisfied my feet and toes were clean it slithered higher, across my calf, circling around my leg, touching every inch of it. The only sound in the open air was my calm breath and the drip and slide of the sponge.

Next up were my thighs, as thorough as he had been with the rest of my legs he washed them as well. Slowly and softly it cleansed me of all my worries. It didn't particularly linger on any space, it just washed me in deliberate and respectful movement. It wasn't a sexual experience, it was more of an unwinding occurrence.

It caressed between my legs with a feathery light touch. Higher and higher the tentacles stroked me with that soft, soapy sponge. My back soon followed my stomach. One big tentacle circled around my waist, touching and washing me wherever it touched.

It washed my breasts and my nipples that had gone soft again in the warm water. With a sweep of the sponge my nipples puckered up again and a tremor of pleasure shot through me. But it didn't linger, it went higher and washed my arms one by one, stretching me out as if an offering, but only to be able to get every inch of me soaped in with that sponge. Each finger got a swipe of its own, it even got the dirt from underneath my fingernails.

A squirting sound made my eyes pop open. It had taken my shampoo bottle and squirted a royal amount on two of its tentacles. I closed my eyes again, letting the creature take over. The comforting familiar smell of my minty shampoo filled my senses. It mixed with the citrus scent of the yuzu limes, creating a delicious new fragrant.

Four tentacles touched my head, washing my hair lovingly with slow circular movements. It went from scalp to tip and back up again, massaging and washing my hair. After that, it washed out each strand of my hair until all the remaining soap had dissipated. Next up it lathered my silky hair in conditioner, massaging it in every strand. It rinsed all of the product out, leaving my hair floating in a cloud around my head.

I sighed in contentment, this indeed was the most relaxing hot spring or even wellness I had ever been to.

After every inch of me was as clean as it could be, it started massaging my aching muscles. It started on my feet again, massaging away the age of the thousands of footsteps I had taken. My calves had strained with every step and staircase. My thighs had carried me for miles on end. My lower back had carried my backpack. My sides had hurt after a particularly straining climb. My shoulders that had carried the weight of it all and, lastly my neck. It felt like all the tension that it had massaged out had gathered at my neck.

It teased away any and all of the strain lurking away underneath my skin. Again the touch was not sensual, it was more respectful and oriented focus than I had experienced before. It kneaded my muscles, touching me in multiple places at once.

Every knot it could find it massaged out, every touch felt like a weight lifted off me. Where I had some real knots in my muscles, it used its suction cups to search my pressure points and make it release itself. Every knot and ache disappeared under its caring touch.

My body felt like overcooked noodles. Never before had I felt so at ease in my own skin. It was almost as if it had remade me into a new person. The only place that hadn't been attended as thoroughly too, was between my legs. With all of the soft caresses, I felt myself getting aroused, but it seemed disrespectful to bring it up. Already this creature had done more for me to heal my ailments than any type of medicine and sleep could do.

Almost as if it could sense my thoughts, the tentacles started to move again. Its actions were more deliberate this time, focusing on specific places on my body that only heightened my arousal.

The soles of my feet and palms of my hands were grasped and touched in a sensual way, caressing me like a lover's touch. Another pair of tentacles circled my inner thighs, spreading open my legs, but not touching between. One big tentacle circled my waist, giving me pressure on my lower back and belly in the best way possible. It squeezed me, making me gasp, and shivers of delight coursed through my body.

Higher up my body, my shoulders, neck, and ears were being rubbed. The tentacle moved over my shoulder, circling them, touching the sides of my breasts. It lifted my upper body a bit higher so my breasts peaked out of the water again. The cold air made my nipples tighten and my breasts ache. It circled my breasts, pushing them higher to create a makeshift bra. It was as if it was presenting my breasts as an offering to the cool air while the rest of my body remained in the warm water.

Two tentacles slithered over my breasts, focusing on my neglected nipples. Suction cups fixed around them, pulsating and massaging in a way that made my whole body tremble. It almost felt like two tiny mouths were sucking on my nipples. The tentacles around my breast repeated the same rhythmic squeezing and pulsating. My breasts felt like living beings, woken up by a dance and a piece of music that only the creature could hear.

One tentacle pushed up into the air. The splashing sound made my eyes open. I looked at it, waiting to see what it would do. After what seemed like the most pleasurable of eternities, it slowly descended to my body. Between my breasts, over my belly, lower and lower it slithered. The air had cooled it a bit, so it was in stark contrast with my hot skin. Reaching its final destination between my legs, it finally touched my one neglected spot. My pussy was pulsing with need, ready to be stroked, filled, and fucked by this creature.

The tentacle teased me, stroking around my pussy, touching my outer lips, but not yet slipping between them. I moaned loudly, ready to beg for it to fill me, but a tentacle slid over my mouth silencing me. Sticking out my tongue, I licked the salty, wet appendix. The water of the hot spring wasn't salty, but its skin was. A shiver went through it, and immediately it latched onto my clit. The same rhythmic music pattern used on my breasts began to play on my clit. It felt like a tiny mouth sucking on me and my eyes shot open.

I could see myself absolutely surrounded by the monster. Multiple tentacles embodied me and even more rose out of the water to touch and stroke me. I closed my eyes again, reveling in the feel of their peculiar texture on my skin.

One end pushed at my entrance at the same time as another requested entry of my mouth. I opened my lips accepting it, and it slid inside at the same time as it breached my core. The movement at my clit ceased as it slowly but surely filled my pussy with the most exquisite feeling ever. It didn't feel like anything I had experienced before. The texture was squishy and soft, but also unwavering as it pushed inside of me, slowly stretching me to accommodate more of it.

It felt like an endless experience as it filled me, twisting inside of me as if trying to fit as much of it as it could. My muscles squeezed around it. The tentacle inside my mouth touched my tongue, willing it to come out and play. I licked it back and a slow dance of seduction happened in my mouth at the same time as I was being stuffed to the brink in my pussy.

Just when I thought that I couldn't take more, it stilled its movements. I had no idea how much of it was inside, but my body had stretched deliciously to accommodate it. A soft pressure from inside against my front wall made me gasp around the tentacle in my mouth. My smothered noises filled the silent evening.

It touched me in the most pleasurable spot inside of me. The little sucker at my clit that had been silent until now suddenly started sucking again. In tandem, it massaged me in the same spot inside and outside. Pleasure raked my body and the climax that had been building up washed over me.

All at once, all the tentacles started to move and caress me. Like a beautiful dance, my whole body was being pleasured by the rhythmic movements of the creature. It massaged my breasts, and sucked my nipples into little suction cups, acting as mouths. The tentacle in my mouth started its dance of seduction again and I was helpless against it, reacting as I should. The tentacle inside of me started to thrust, creating the most delicious of friction while the one on my clit increased its suckling pressure.

Pressure at my back entrance made my back arch, but my body didn't move much as it was being held down by multiple tentacles. I relaxed and it breached my ass with just a bit of pressure. It stretched my virgin asshole slowly but deliberately. Inch after inch slid inside of me, more than I ever imagined I could take. The pressure inside of me built as more of it slid inside of me.

The creature filled me in every imaginable way and pleasured me in ways that made my body respond with every movement. The waves of pleasure didn't stop, each thrust, each flick, each suck only augmented my ongoing orgasm. My whole body felt like it was designed for this one purpose, being pleasured by this magnificent creature.

It twisted its tentacles inside of me, turning them in a way that made my eyes roll back. It twisted and twisted until it suddenly stopped. My breathing caught when I felt two suckers inside of me, meet each other through the tin membrane separating both my holes. More suckers awoke, it seemed to have twisted its tentacles so that the suckers were on the outside, caressing my inner walls. For a moment it stilled its movement, letting me catch my breath before it started to suck on me from all directions.

Wave after wave of pleasure washed over me, sensations filled my body and brain in a way that I could almost feel overloaded with the enormity of the experience. The biggest and longest orgasm of my life took over my body, trembling and squeezing in the same rhythmic dance as the creature.

When I felt like my brain couldn't keep up with the sensations of my body, it slowly stilled its movements, letting me come down from the amazing high it had pushed me to.

First, the tentacle in my mouth slid out, letting me take a big gulp of breath. Immediately it offered me a refreshing sip of water which I gladly took. Then the tentacle in my ass slid out, leaving behind a delicious burn. It returned with some soothing balm it comfortingly spread on my used hole. Lastly, the one in my pussy slid out in a circular motion, caressing my inner walls as it exited, leaving pleasurable tremors in its wake.

No longer stuffed, I could feel my body coming down. One by one the tentacles across my body caressed me and released me, letting me float in the comforting water.

This had been the most relaxing experience of my life. I knew with one hundred percent certainty that I would go back to Kurokawa Onsen to visit this bathhouse and this magnificent creature.

"Thank you," I mumbled.

It was my pleasure, Ava.

The End

Courted by El Sombrerón

This is not how I imagined my vacation to Guatemala to go. Spellbound sitting in my hotel bed, unable to move while El Sombrerón braided my hair.

I should have declined his advances as soon as they started, but I kinda liked the attention of a handsome local man. If I had realized he was the legendary El Sombrerón, I would have never responded to his courting. But now it was too late. As soon as he finished the braid, I would be his bride for eternity.

At least then I would have someone that cared for me. I had been alone for so long, so when someone paid attention to me, especially a dark and handsome man, I responded to it immediately.

I had fallen for him like a bird out of its nest. The late-night serenades, the walks under the moonlight, and his charming compliments had made me feel like I was the prettiest girl in the world. Nobody ever noticed me besides my long brown locks. It had been the first thing to attract him, but his compliments and charm had grown and not only focused on my hair.

The sweet old lady at the hotel had tried to warn me of the legend, but it had been too late. I was under his enchantment, and I would have let him ravish me that night. I just hadn't expected a spell and marriage proposal.

"Soon you will be ready for my cock, my bride."

His deep, southing voice took me out of my thoughts. I gasped, not yet used to his forwardness. A shiver went through my body and my thighs clenched together. I couldn't move, but I could still use my lips to tell him off.

"What if I don't want your cock?"

The words might have sounded more convincing if I didn't say them so breathlessly. My body betrayed me by gathering wetness between my legs to make for easy entrance of his cock. The soft touch of his hands in my hair made my stomach flutter. He was so caring and dominating at the same time. He leaned closer and I could feel his muscular chest against my almost naked back. I was still only wearing the bikini I had put on to go to the beach. The softness of the fabric of his black shirt caressed me like a lover's touch.

"I will make sure that you do. I will make you beg for it," El Sombrerón whispered in my ear in a sultry tone that made my heart skip a beat.

His voice had been the first thing that had drawn me to him. I had heard him sing in the streets of the village I was visiting, and I felt entranced by his southing tone and delicious accent. I should have known then that he was no ordinary man.

"By using magic?"

His low chuckle vibrated through me. He licked the shell of my ear and the shiver that followed flowed to my pussy. His warm breath smelled like mint and tobacco, a combination I truly enjoyed.

"No magic needed, my love, only my hands, and my mouth."

El Sombrerón was using magic to immobilize my body, but it seemed that my body reacting, was all me. In my mind, I knew I had to resist more, but then again, what was the point?

"You know you can always say no, my sweet bride."

I closed my eyes, nodding. He hadn't coerced me in any way; he had just seduced me, courted me, and made me fall in love with him. I didn't know which one was worse.

"Why me?" I asked, hating how much my voice trembled.

I could feel the careless shrug of his shoulder behind me. The fabric caressed my almost naked back sensually.

"Why not you?"

I hated that answer. There had been so many other more beautiful girls on the street that night, but he had picked me. I needed to know why. I shook my head, his hand letting go of the nearly finished braid.

"Why not pick any other girl, then?"

El Sombrerón made an unhappy sound behind me.

"You understand me wrong, my love. Why would I not pick you? You have the most beautiful big eyes and the softest brown hair, and your voice makes me feel things inside I haven't for eternity. When I approached you, instead of looking away, you gave me the gift of your smile."

My lips curled into a smile. He had a way with words that made me like putty in his hands. He started his slow methodical braiding again, and I relaxed in his touch. Why not me? Why should I not enjoy what is happening? He cared for me, and I felt that I was starting to care for him as well.

At the end of my braid, his hands stilled.

"May I finish the braid, my bride?"

The question meant more than just the simple act of putting the band on the end of the tail. It would mean being bonded to him forever. Becoming his bride, and this would start our wedding night.

"Yes."

My voice almost didn't sound like my own. It had a husky quality to it I hadn't heard before. Almost as if that one word begged him to make me his in all ways possible.

He put the finishing touches on the braid and I could feel a zing pass through me. I could move my limbs again, but I enjoyed leaning against him. His hands, no longer focused on my hair, caressed my back, loosening the bikini straps.

I closed my eyes and let him touch me in all the ways he wanted. I wanted it as well. He had a soft, caring touch that I needed to feel. With every caress, a shiver went through me.

"You're mine now, my love."

El Sombrerón discarded the scraps of fabric and I sat naked on the bed with him behind me. His strong muscular chest touched my naked back, and I reveled in the warmth that radiated from him. At least I would have someone to keep me warm on cold winter nights.

His hands massaged my shoulders. He took his time and care to make me as relaxed as possible. I could feel all the tension of the day melt away under his gentle touch. After he was satisfied with my shoulders, he carefully touched my arms, pausing for a breath before he circled them around me.

I felt safe and cherished in his embrace. When I didn't protest his hug, he cupped my breasts. I made a soft noise of pleasure, which encouraged him to start rubbing my nipples with the palms of his hands while kneading my breasts with his big fingers. My nipples hardened and sparks of pleasure burst underneath my eyelids like little firecrackers.

The low rumble in his chest vibrated through me. He hummed the same song he had serenaded me with the night we met underneath the moonlight.

The vibrations intensified the pleasurable feeling in my breasts that he massaged rhythmically.

I bit my lip to keep from moaning. Just when I was about to beg him to fuck me, to fill me, to make me truly his, his hands started to decent. He stroked the undersides of my breasts, moving lower over my rounded stomach, slowly caressing my hips and thighs. He didn't mind them being more than a handful. Then he spread my legs in one swift movement that made me gasp. I let my head fall back on his shoulder. Immediately, he laved my neck with his tongue, making shivers course through me. Wetness gathered between my legs and I could feel my thighs quiver.

I wanted him. No, I needed him inside of me as I had never needed anything before.

So very slowly, as if prolonging the moment as long as he could, he slid his hand in between my legs. I was wet and ready for him. He teased the outline of my pussy with one finger as if to map it out so he could paint a picture of it later. Or maybe he would write a song about it. I wanted to ask him, but just then he slid the finger lower, dipping inside of me. A breathless sigh of pleasure filled the room, while he touched me in my most intimate spot. His other hand gripped my thigh and his tail the other, keeping my legs open as in an offering for him.

Slowly, he pushed in and pulled out. Each time he entered me, my muscles squeezed around his finger as if to keep him inside. He gathered my moisture and lifted his finger. I opened my eyes just in time to see him suck on that wet finger.

"Delicious," he said in a deep, raspy voice.

Seeing my juices disappear into that sexy mouth did something to me. I moaned, craning my neck, almost touching my lips to his.

"Kiss me," I breathed out.

The fire in his eyes could consume me. It would be our first kiss and I wanted it to be one to remember. He licked his lips, eliciting another moan out of me before he descended, his mouth on mine. His lips felt soft, and he tasted like coffee and tobacco with a hint of peppermint. He opened his mouth, letting out his tongue, requesting me access. I opened mine and when our tongues touched, I could almost see the sparks fly between us. It was electrifying in a way I had never felt before. His tongue caressed mine, deepening the kiss and making me forget about everything else.

His hands refocused on my most intimate spot while he devoured my mouth. El Sombrerón spread open my pussy with one hand while circling my clit with the other. I sighed with pleasure, loving the way he made me feel. He kissed me in a way that made my toes curl while he stroked my clit at just the right pace. Slow circles alternating with a little flick up and down. I could feel my pleasure build and knew it wouldn't be long before I shattered.

I raised my hands and I could feel him still in his movements, waiting to see what I would do. I mewled in discontent and pushed my hips up to encourage him. He began his ministrations of my body again after I teased my tongue on him. Raising my hands to his head, I grasped his thick black hair to deepen the kiss.

He growled in appreciation and reacted to me with a passion that took my breath away. Not once did he stop circling and touching my clit. My arousal grew and became bigger with his slow and steady strokes. Suddenly, I could feel my body tightening and releasing the pressure all at once. Pleasure flowed through me in waves and I had to stop kissing him to be able to catch my breath. A scream of pleasure tore from my mouth and my whole body trembled with the aftershocks.

El Sombrerón stopped his assault on my clit and slowly caressed me to let me come down from my pleasure.

I looked at him and saw the love and devotion I felt reflected in his dark eyes. With a tilt of my chin, I requested another kiss, which he happily gave me. He devoured my mouth again as a man starved, discovering every inch of it and making it all his.

He broke off the kiss to stand up from the bed. He was still fully clothed while I was completely naked. I bit my lip, admiring his physique, not really believing he was mine.

His black shiny boots clicked on the floor as he took a few steps forward. With swift movements he discarded his silky black shirt. He lowered his hands to his thick, black, shiny belt that hid away the treasure he had. The black and white signature Sombrero hat he always wore had been casually thrown to the side at the beginning of the evening. I could see his tail trashing around as if impatient. His olive skin glinted in the moonlight shining through the windows.

This magnificent man was all mine, and I drank in his appearance, memorizing every detail of him. Besides his tail and pointy teeth, he looked very human. His face was classically handsome, with a powerful jaw and kissable lips. His dark eyes shot fire revealing his power inside. He could be a dangerous man if you crossed him in the wrong way. But his fire was directed at me in the most pleasurable way.

It was the dead of night and quiet outside. The moonlight that had encompassed us when we met hugged us like a blanket. It almost felt like we were the only two people awake at this time of night, ready to seal our bond.

El Sombrerón undressed with confident movements. As soon as all his clothes were discarded, he crawled onto the bed with me. Naked in all his glory, I wasn't able to pull my eyes from his massive cock dangling between his legs. I wasn't sure it was going to fit, but I sure as hell wanted to find out.

Spreading my legs, I expected him to just get to the main attraction, but he dived in between them with his head. He licked me, sucked me, and caressed me with his tongue. Pleasuring me until my back arched from the bed and I was begging for his cock, just as he had predicted.

"Please, I need you."

"I will give you everything you need, my sweet Bride."

He dove back in between, torturing me with his talented tongue. El Sombrerón circled my clit, flicked it, sucked on it, and did everything he could to make me go crazy. He let me tether on the edge of my orgasm, not giving me the release I so desperately craved.

"I need your cock," I moaned, not believing those words came out of my mouth.

El Sombrerón looked up with a wicked smile, his lips glinting with my juices and his eyes burning with the fire of his passion.

"You ask and I shall give it to you, my love."

I grabbed his shoulders to pull him up, and he let me. There was no way I could move his massive frame, but he let me guide him to where I needed him. His big body covered mine, and I loved the feeling of his impressive body over mine. It made me feel small and feminine and protected in a way I hadn't experienced before. His chest hair tickled my nipples, only heightening my arousal. I couldn't stop the needy little sounds escaping me if I tried.

I opened my legs wide, gripped his cock, and slid it between my pussy lips. I coated his cock in my juices, pressing it against my clit, loving the feel of him. My wetness eased the entry and, with a solid thrust, he pushed into me. My muscles stretched and gripped him tight, never before having been so full. Sounds came out of my mouth that sounded foreign to me, but were all the result of this connection. I felt whole, complete, like the missing piece of the puzzle finally found its place.

"Fuck, you feel perfect, my sweet bride," he said in a loving tone.

He gave me a moment to get used to his size, mumbling sweet nothingness the whole time to make me relax around him. When I didn't feel like I was going to rip apart anymore, he slowly started moving. He stretched me with every thrust in the most delicious of ways.

"Yes, please harder," I begged.

"Everything for you, my love," he said, thrusting into me harder.

Every movement ignited sparks of pleasure inside of me, building up to something bigger. I touched him everywhere I could, his muscular chest, his bread shoulders, his silky hair. I felt connected to him at this moment and I wanted to share it with him in a way that transcended words. Looking into his eyes, I could see that he felt the same way. It was strange to feel so much already for someone I had only just met, but it felt right.

I met him thrust for thrust, loving the way he growled each time he bottomed out inside of me. I wanted to come, but I just needed a little something more. As if he could read my mind, his tail pushed in between us and started circling around my clit, giving me just what I required to reach that edge.

"Yes, just like that," I moaned out loud.

Not caring that my voice carried outside the window into the night, I moaned his name over and over again. Anyone passing by may hear how good my El Sombrerón is taking me.

Pleasure like nothing I had ever experienced washed over me. My muscles squeezed around him and his thrusts grew sloppy and wilder.

"Mine," he growled, his more animalistic side coming out for a second.

The sounds he made only spurred me on more. I let out a gasp of pleasure, digging my nails into his shoulders. He shouted out in pleasure as he pumped one last time before his cock throbbed and his seed filled me, completing our bond. I could feel him shuddering, my muscles squeezing around him, milking every last bit of his release.

He collapsed on top of me, and I enjoyed feeling his weight. Soothingly I stroked his shoulders and back, trying to catch my breath, mesmerized by the feel of our connection.

My life would never be the same. I would be the wife of a bogeyman, but I noticed that I didn't mind it. I had no idea what was in store for me and how our worlds would match, but I wanted to experience it with him, El Sombrerón, my husband. My vacation in Guatemala ended differently than how I had expected, but in no way was that bad.

We discovered each other bodies all evening with much pleasure. We still have all our lives to discover each other hearts, but I felt already more connected to him than I have ever been before.

The End

Saved by the Yeti

This sucks. I didn't even like skiing and now I was trapped in a heap of snow, darkness closing in while I could have been at home with a nice cup of cocoa.

But no, I had to be cool and go on this stupid ski trip. Ugh. Fucking FOMO. I was going to die, and it was all my own dumb fault. I didn't know how to ski, but I didn't want to be the only one not to go along on the annual company trip.

As my last thought was filled with regret at taking the job that had landed me here, darkness and coldness seeped in.

THE NEXT SENSATION was warmth. I opened my eyes, and snow no longer surrounded me. I was in a cozy cave with a crisp fire burning that warmed my cold bones. With a shiver, I crawled closer and noticed the soft furs that covered me. A bit primitive, but I was definitely not complaining since it had saved my life. Another shiver shook my body when I realized just how close I had been to death.

Movement at the entrance of the cave drew my attention. A massive white form filled the entryway and blocked out the light and wind from outside. My brain tried to register what I was seeing, but it had coped with too much in a too short time period. I passed out. The last thought on my mind was that the big, bulky form must belong to my savior.

WHEN I WOKE UP AGAIN, more warmth surrounded me. After opening my eyes, I noticed that the fire had died out, but I was still super toasty. As my brain tried to catch up, I noticed that the heat was coming from behind me and that

I was naked. Survival one o one, of course, taking off wet clothes to make sure someone doesn't freeze to death, but who or what had taken off my clothes? I didn't remember doing it myself.

I tried to turn around to look at the source of heat behind me, but I couldn't because a massive arm was restricting my way. White, soft fur covered the colossal arm. A giant creature spooned me. Instead of panicking like a normal person, I sighed in contentment. I could have died, so being hugged by a warm, soft, and furry monster was really not the worst.

Slowly I became aware of my body. My fingers and toes still tingled from the freezing cold that I almost hadn't escaped from. I was completely naked, but I didn't appear to be harmed in any way. The smell of the died-out fire filled my senses, and combined with it was the scent of leather and wet animal. All in all, not the most pleasant of sensations to wake up to, but also not the worst.

Considering I couldn't move, I studied my surroundings. First, I inspected the gigantic furry white arm that covered the front of my body and held me snugly against the toasty oven at my back. My head rested on the biceps of the other arm as a pillow. The hair seemed clean, soft, and well taken care of. At the end of the arm was a huge hand, almost bigger than my head. I counted five fingers, so not so different from mine, besides the size.

I felt... safe, and secure in the enormous arms of the unknown creature that had saved my life. The toastiness level also helped, as it was such a stark contrast with the cold I had escaped from. Studying its fingers more closely, I imagined how they might feel inside of me, and I had to bite my lip to suppress a moan. I wanted to see its face and put a visual on my savior. When I tried to turn around; its grip tightened, rubbing my sensitive nipples beneath its big palm. They immediately hardened under its touch. I gasped and stilled my movements, listening to hear if its breathing had changed, but it remained calm, deep asleep.

I squirmed again, but the only result was that I became aware of something else. There was a giant erection behind me, pressing against my ass. So definitely a he. Gasping, I could feel my body responding. My muscles tightened around emptiness and wetness started to gather between my legs. My hard nipples puckered and pressed into his palm, begging for more friction.

If anything was beneficial to a girl's libido, it was a near-death experience. Lust surged through me, all directed at the creature behind me. Without it,

I would have frozen to death and my body found only in the summer when everything thawed.

I wiggled a bit more until his erection slipped between my legs. God, I wanted to see it so badly, but the massive arm blocked my view. I was so focused on the feeling of his giant cock between my legs that I didn't notice his breathing change.

Moving my hips to create some friction between the cock and my pussy, I could feel myself getting wet. If only I could find the right angle to...

A low, dangerous growl behind me made me still my movements. My breathing caught in my throat. I hoped the creature was friendly.

"What you doing?" the monster grunted at my back.

His voice was rough as if he hadn't used it in a while. The deep timbre of it vibrated through my chest. His warm breath tickled my hair and his scent enveloped me. He smelled of a mix of animal hide and fire. I closed my eyes and focused on my feelings, totally shutting off my common sense.

"I want you," I moaned as I rubbed myself against its erection. "Please, let me feel alive."

He growled behind me. A sound so absolutely masculine and animalistic that I groaned in response. He let his massive hand move down over my belly to between my legs. His rough fingers left a trail of goose bumps in its path. I was wet and when his fingers discovered my moisture, it grunted again, more pleased.

"This what you want?" he asked as he slid one of his meaty fingers inside of me.

His finger alone was as big as some men's cocks. My muscles squeezed around it and I moaned in pleasure. His other hand encompassed my breast and started to massage it in rough but pleasurable movements.

"More," I begged.

I let my hand slide down and I gripped his rock-hard cock. My hand couldn't even fully encompass its width. He felt impossibly big, but I wanted it inside of me. He grunted again and pushed his hips up. I stroked it up and down as much as I could. Cupping both my hands, I enveloped its head, twisting around, earning pleasurable sounds from the monster behind me.

"I give you what you want," it said.

After a few more thrusts with his finger, he let it slide out of me. A disappointed sound left me, but turned into a moan of delight when he lifted my leg over his hip. His soft fur tickled the inside of my thigh and made pleasurable tremors rake through my body. He moved his hips, coating his cock with my juices and making me quiver with anticipation. When I was almost ready to beg for it, he gave me all of him. With the right hip movement, he slid into me with one thrust. My pussy stretched to accommodate it, but it fit just perfectly. I let my head fall back on his shoulder and moaned in pleasure.

"More," I whispered.

I wanted it all. I wanted to feel alive again, to forget what had happened, and to surrender completely to the pleasure my rescuer was giving me.

He seemed to understand what I needed, because he gripped my leg tighter, slowly withdrew, and thrust into me again harder than before. He gave me the exact pounding that I needed to be able to forget about everything else and focus only on his massive cock inside of me.

The sounds that came from my throat seemed like they were not made by me. I sounded like a woman on the edge of the precipice who didn't care who was fucking her and how she was going to fall. I wanted him to fall with me, I wanted to give him the same type of pleasure that he was giving me.

Arching my back, I presented my breasts to his gaze. I let one of my hands slide to them while I gripped his fur with the other. I squeezed his arm encouraging while I flicked my hard nipple, moaning with pleasure. The sharp intake of his breath, followed by the low growl, sounded through the small space of the cave. He gripped me tighter and quickened his pace.

"This what you want?" he growled as he thrust into me hard and fast.

I closed my eyes, enjoying the onslaught of pleasure on my body. He touched all the right points inside of me to get me to that climax in no time. Quivers of pleasure shot through me. My pussy pulsed and gripped his cock with each thrust he delivered.

"Yes," I panted.

I felt alive with this amazing creature inside of me. Almost as if I could take on the world, as long as I had him. My orgasm was building deep inside of me and I felt like this would be a climax that was going to change my worldview and my view of monsters as a whole. I was never a monster hater or a monster fucker, but now it seemed that I had chosen my camp in the best of ways. My climax grew, and I wanted to experience it with him. I wanted to push him over that edge with me.

"More," I moaned. "Fill me, take me, fuck me, breed me."

I knew that that last one would tip him over. No monster could ignore its primal need to breed a female. He cursed roughly behind me and the grip on my hip tightened. I knew I was going to get a bruise from it and I loved it marking me as his.

"You want me to fill you with my seed? Breed Yeti babies in you?" he grunted low and almost angry.

"Yes, yes!" I screamed out in joy.

I did want this. I wanted everything he could give me. I wanted to be filled by him as I had never been filled before. I wanted him to lose his control and make me completely his. I didn't know where those thoughts came from, but it felt right.

"Breed me!" I moaned.

I felt him quiver behind me, vibrations coursing through me, and I heard his low growl fill the cave. He wasn't going to last long. My own orgasm wasn't far off, and I wanted to reach it together with him. My hand that had been playing with my nipple slid lower and found my clit. With just a bit of pressure, my orgasm shot off.

"Yes, yes, I'm coming," I exclaimed as I felt the first waves of pleasure flow through my body.

My body stiffened, and my muscles squeezed together around him.

With a groan, he let go as well, and I felt his cock throb inside me and fill me with his seed. My orgasm lengthened and seemed to last as long as his. He vibrated inside me and I felt the last spurt of cum inside me. A warm feeling spread inside me with the knowledge that he had marked my insides as his own.

With that final thought, I fell asleep in the warm embrace of the Yeti that had saved me, with his cock still deep inside of me.

I WOKE UP WITH THE sensation of something warm and wet between my legs. I looked up and saw the front of the Yeti for the first time. It was magnificent, kneeling between my legs with his face buried in my pussy.

He looked up, sensing my eyes on him. Big blue eyes gazed into mine and I could see kindness in them. His face was rough, almost ape-like with white fur covering his cheekbones and forehead. I wanted to touch him, and thank him for saving me, but I also didn't want him to stop doing what he had been doing when I woke up.

"Thank you," I said, with a raspy voice.

He grunted and focused on my glistening pussy again. I could feel myself becoming even wetter with his penetrating eyes on me. His seed was dripping out, making a mess of the furs, but I didn't care.

"Wait," I said before he started to lick me again and all rational thought would disappear from my mind. "What is your name?"

"Jens," he grunted and bowed low again. After a swipe of its tongue that made my back arch of the fur, he looked up again. "You?"

"Hmm," I responded, almost lightheaded from pleasure.

He had the biggest tongue I had ever seen and felt before. It was twice as wide as my hand, and with that one lick, he had touched everything. I had to compose myself before I was able to answer that simple question.

"I'm Evelyn. Thank you for saving me, Jens," I said.

"You mine now," he grunted and went to work on my pussy.

His words made something clench inside. His? I wanted to be his in all ways, but could I? My rational thoughts vanished when his massive, talented tongue touched my pussy and clit in the best ways. I wouldn't mind waking up like this every day.

He licked me as if I was his breakfast and he had been starving for a long time. His immense tongue seemed to touch every pleasure point I had, making my toes curl. Sounds of pleasure left my mouth with each delicious sweep of his tongue. He made of point of trying to elicit even more noise from me, rumbling happily every time I did.

Soon I was gasping and moaning on the edge of an orgasm, ready for him to take me, but he didn't. He kept licking and tasting me as if he had all the time in the world.

"Please Jens, I need you," I moaned.

He looked up, cocking his head and studying my face. His fingers took over the task of his tongue and he entered me, stretching me in the best way, but it wasn't enough.

"You have me," he said matter-of-factly.

"I need more," I whispered, my voice raspy with emotion.

He pushed another finger inside of me, stretching me more. Pumping in and out, he gave me the right amount of friction, but after having experienced his cock, I craved it. Lifting my hips, I met every one of his thrusts, hoping he would make me go over the edge. He studied me, licking his lips clean of the juices he had sucked up. Seeing his tongue work in his mouth, made a low, needy noise escape me. I felt like a wanton woman, but I needed all of him.

"Please," I begged. "I need you inside of me."

He looked down at where his fingers were entering me. I sighed. I really was going to need to spell it out for this big Yeti.

"I need your cock."

His eyes shot up to my face, his gaze filled with passion. He pushed up and I could finally see his cock. It was massive. If he hadn't already fucked me with it, I would have never believed it would fit. I had felt how thick he was, but I had no idea that he was as long as my forearm. He gripped it, giving it a few strokes, grunting in that delicious masculine and animalistic way that made me all hot and bothered. I couldn't take my eyes off him. He inched closer, slowly as if to give me time to say no. I wasn't going to say no. I wanted this, I wanted him. I wanted to be his.

I opened my legs wide to welcome him. He knelt in between them, pushing forward until his fat head rested on my pussy. It looked almost comically big in comparison to my small hole. He rubbed the head between my pussy lips, coating it in my juices, making me mewl in pleasure.

"Please, I need you," I moaned.

He looked into my eyes and the emotions I saw in them made me catch my breath. I had been so focused on my own feelings of pleasure and desire that I didn't think that it would mean more for him, but his eyes told me otherwise.

"You mine," he grunted. "We make yeti babies together. You stay."

I nodded, not trusting my voice to break with the emotions that whirled through me. I had never had anyone look at me the way he was now as if I was his entire world.

He seemed content with my agreement and focused on my pussy again. He grabbed his thick cock and slowly pushed it inside of me. After a little resistance, I could feel my entrance opening up and he slid inside of me. I moaned, enjoying the feel of my big Yeti stretching me to the max. He pushed further and further, but only half of him was inside of me when he reached my limit. I gasped and writhed, trying to take more of him, but I couldn't. He thrust shallowly, but I could see that he wanted more.

"Wait," I said.

I pushed his chest gently, but he growled in disagreement.

"We can fit more in a different position," I assured him.

After a moment of hesitation and another unsatisfying shallow thrust, he pulled out. The part that had been inside of me glistened with my juices and I had to bite my lip from leaning forward and licking it all off. I would have time for that later.

I moved sideways and crawled on my hands and knees, presenting my ass to him. Looking behind me, I could see he appreciated the view. The low growl he emitted confirmed it. I angled my butt up and let my head rest on the soft furs that smelled like him. I opened my mouth to give him instructions, but the feel of his big hands on my ass cheeks silenced me. My Yeti knew what to do and soon I could feel him push at my entrance.

Slowly and surely, he filled me up, inch after inch of his exquisite cock. I stretched to accommodate him, never before had I felt so full. It felt like he went on for ages. The stretch and burn made me gasp in pleasure. Just when I thought I couldn't take more, that he had filled me beyond my breaking point, I could feel his hips touch my ass cheeks. He had bottomed out inside of me and it felt heavenly.

Sounds I didn't recognize fled my mouth, encouraging him to move. His fingers gripped my hips tightly. He pulled out slowly and thrust into me in one hard motion. I cried out in pleasure and he moved again, pumping in and out of me, making me take every inch of him. His balls slapped my clit and with every thrust, I could feel the pleasure grow inside of me. I grabbed the fur to be able to have something to hold onto, and I let myself enjoy the ride.

His growls of pleasure bounced off the walls and I knew it wouldn't be long before he filled me up again. My own orgasm wasn't far off, and I wanted him to lose control and make me fully his.

"Yes, Jens. Breed me!"

His snarl would have scared me if I hadn't seen the love and devotion in his eyes. He thrust into me faster and harder. Each slide of his cock only augmented my pleasure and made me rush to the finish line faster. I was a moaning mess. My walls clenched around him, setting off my climax. My body trembled, muscles spasmed and pleasurable sounds were ripped from my throat. I could feel him pulse inside of me, ready to release his load.

"Fill me up with yeti babies. Make me yours!" I screamed in the throes of my orgasm.

It was enough to set him off as well.

"Mine!"

He growled and snarled, thrusting in a few last times, before he filled me with his seed, breeding me and making me his.

My knees buckled, and I collapsed, a twitching orgasmic mess of a person. He followed me behind, careful not to crush me. He lay beside me, pulling me into his warm embrace. Surrounded by his arms, I felt safe and loved.

The End

Mated to a Vampire

"**I**ntruder spotted on the western perimeter," I said through my link to my Pack.

In wolf form, I ran across the perimeter, chasing the scent I had picked up. It had drawn me somehow. I couldn't explain it, but I needed to find the source of that smell.

Mate! Piped a voice in the back of my head.

I resolutely ignored it. I'm pretty sure my mate won't be some intruder. Maybe it will be the son of an Alpha from one of my neighboring territories. As a solitaire Luna at the head of my pack, I was starting to get lonely. I had plenty of sex of course, but the bond with a Mate transcended that and everything else. He would need to be strong to rule beside me. Perhaps with dark fur, to offset my white. Fierce, intelligent, fast, worthy of being my Mate.

Dreaming of my future Mate, almost made me pass by him. He had cleverly hidden his tracks with animal dung, but somehow his smell perpetrated all of that. It was hard to pinpoint. The scent was almost sickly sweet, with a hint of something coppery mixed with a delicious musky flavor. It was the most delectable thing I had ever smelled.

I stopped, sniffed in the air, and followed the trail. He was smart, but he wasn't as familiar with this territory as I was. I grew up here, and I knew every branch, every bush, and every sound these woods made. And I knew when something was off. I changed to my human form, to be a smaller target, and creep up on him.

Arriving at a clearing, I could see him washing off his scent in the small stream. Another smart move, but it would have been smarter to keep moving. I slowly approached, not making a sound, studying my prey. I could only see his powerful, athletic back. His muscles worked while he tore off his shirt, splashing water on himself to soften his delicious scent.

His dark hair was a bit too long, perfect for running my hands through while he thrust into me. I shook my head, trying to get the erotic thoughts out of my head. I mean, I love sex as much as the next gall, but this was getting unprofessional.

My stupid movement had drawn his attention. In a flash, he whirled around and bared his pointy teeth. A fucking Vamp. In my territory? Hell no!

"Well, aren't you a pretty face? Too bad I have to smash it for crossing my borders," I growled, raising my fists.

He held up his hands, protecting his ridiculously handsome face. His red eyes enhanced his pale, royal cheekbones. His ruby, biteable lips covered his fangs. His face was distracting me. Maybe I should just hit him, knock him out so I could stare at him. I mean, bring him in. Why would I want to stare at a disgusting vampire? He baled his hands into fists and grinned at me, dancing agile from one side to another.

"Try to touch me, Wolf, and I might bite."

I growled low, a sound that many pups feared, but this Vamp just laughed at me. He actually tilted his chin back and laughed out loud. I used that fraction of a second to jump at him, but he evaded me like it was nothing.

"Too slow," he said with that beautiful smile.

Not beautiful, annoying. I shook my head, trying to get those weird thoughts out of them. It must be some kind of Vampire magic.

"Don't try to charm me, Vamp," I spit out.

He cocked his head, studying me.

"I am not," he said.

I scoffed. Of course he was. Why else would I be fantasizing about biting that smooth, pale neck and putting my mark on it for everyone to see? Vamps were the enemy for as long as any of us could remember. We never mixed and sure as hell never got turned on by the sight of a naked Vampire's chest. His abs looked like they were chiseled from a smooth piece of marble. Visions of my hands running over them, lower and lower until... I shook my head again. Stupid Vamps with stupid charms. It wouldn't work on me. I hadn't been a Luna for over 30 years to get some Vamp to charm my pants off.

While my inner turmoil had distracted me, he veered to the left. I jumped up, trying to grab him, but he danced out of my grip again. Light-footed little bastard, he was. Not so little, of course. He was easily a head taller than me, but he danced away like his height was nothing. As nimble as a squirrel.

He was good. He evaded my every move, but I knew this forest better. I led him to a bush where rabbits used to live underneath. Another evasive maneuver, and his feet got stuck in a sunken rabbit hole. He stumbled, losing his balance for just a fraction of a second, but it was enough for me to jump at him. I wrestled him to the ground, grabbing his hands, and pinning them, while I held him steady with my body.

He tried to wriggle free, but I had the advantage of being on top. His movements suddenly made me become very aware of my naked state. Nudity wasn't a thing to be ashamed of in the pack. I had seen my fair share of naked bodies, but rubbing myself on this Vamp's naked chest made me notice all of our differences. His cold skin sent shivers down my heated body. My nipples puckered, becoming sensitive.

"Stop moving," I said between gritted teeth.

He stilled, and cocked his head again, studying me with his bright red eyes that seemed to look right through me. He licked his lips and grinned, showing his fangs.

"Make me," he said with a voice as smooth as silk.

My body reacted before my brain caught up. I leaned forward, closer and closer, until our lips were just a hair away. His icy breath cooled my lips. A soft growl escaped me before I could stop it. I don't know which one of us broke the distance, but suddenly our mouths met. Hot and cold mingled, passion burst forward, fueling the flame of my desire. We both opened our mouths, letting our tongues out to play. They met in a dance of lust, dueling for dominance neither of us was willing to give up.

If it hadn't been for my crazy good hearing, my Pack might have found me kissing a Vampire. Luckily, I heard my Wolves coming towards us and broke off the kiss.

"What..." he started to say, but I jumped up, grabbing his hands.

"Tie him up and put him in the basement," I yelled at my pack before I pushed him towards them, and then I ran.

IT TOOK ALMOST A WEEK to get over that kiss. A week where I tried everything to get my mind off him, but I couldn't. I even tried sex, but somehow another's touch felt wrong to me. The Vamp must have put some spell on me, and I needed him to get it off.

Approaching the basement, I dismissed my guards. As soon as I entered the closed room, his scent hit me. It was even more potent than when I first smelled it, sweet, male and musky all at once. My body responded to it, my juices started to flow, and that word came back into my mind: *Mate*, purred my Wolf half.

Ignoring that outrageous claim, I walked closer to the cell I held him in. His handsome face looked hollow, his red eyes had lost some of their shine, and the silver chains left angry-looking burn marks across his body.

My heart ached to see him hurt. I had tortured many creatures in my time when they disobeyed rules, but somehow I couldn't stand the sight of the marks on his skin. My footsteps resounded in the silent space.

He lifted his head, his fiery red eyes locked on my face. A ghost of a smile played across his lips.

"Come to finish me off, Luna Cassidy?" he said in a raspy voice.

My name on his lips did something to me that I didn't want to identify. I took a step closer, raising my hand to brush away a strand of his hair, but when he flinched, a sick feeling entered my stomach. Why were our people at war? Why was there so much violence in this world?

I shook my head, trying to get those melancholic thoughts out of my head.

"Just get your spell off of me and I'll be on my way," I said.

His smile disappeared and his eyes fired up. He cocked his head and narrowed his eyes.

"I did not put any spell on you. I was going to say the same thing to you. Bad enough that you animals torture me, but letting a Witch mess with my mind is low even for your kind."

I took a step back as if he had slapped me. His icy word penetrated the fog in my mind. A Witch? Maybe we were being attacked from outside? Taking a step closer I studied him. Vampires were notorious liars, but somehow I trusted his words.

"So you feel it too?"

He scoffed. "I would rather have you kill me than have to admit to being attracted to a Wolf."

I bared my teeth to him snarling, "And I would rather give up my title as Luna than admit to getting turned on by a stinky Vamp."

I took a step closer, and another until we were almost touching. Careful to not touch the silver I lifted a finger to tilt his chin higher. My eyes focused on his mouth. His tongue slid out to wet his ruby-red lips, and a soft growl escaped me.

"Stop messing with my head," I said, my voice breathless.

"Stop messing with mine," he bit back.

I silenced him with a kiss. That was the only reason I did that, I promised myself. Not because I had missed his lips, or wanted another taste him, just to silence him.

Our lips met each other in a spark of fire. I growled, and he moaned, our tongues danced. I let mine slide over one of his fangs. The sharp point nicked me and a drop of blood escaped. He sucked it up as if it was his life link and his moans grew louder. Before I knew it, I had crawled on his lap, capturing his head in my hands while I kissed him like a starved woman. He bit my lip, extracting more blood from me, and I loved it.

I ground down on his lap, and I could feel something hard growing beneath me. Gasping I broke off the kiss. He looked turned on, and angry at the same time. My blood streaked his lips, and with my eyes focused on his mouth, he licked them off. Every drop of my blood disappeared and another pleasurable sound came from him.

"You taste delicious," he said.

His voice was full, lush, and silky again. His eyes burned bright, and I could see his wounds trying to heal, fighting the silver. If only a few drops of my blood, could do that, what would happen when he fully bit me? My core contracted at the thought and I felt wetness gathering between my legs. Why did the thought of him biting me, turn me on so much? If not a spell, then what?

When the bulge underneath me, became even harder, I got up. I had to get out of here before I did something I would regret forever. Like letting him bite me, fuck him, and marking him as mine. *Mine*, the wolf in me growled. Shaking my head again I ran outside. I felt like a wet dog, with the number of times I was shaking my head to clear my thoughts. Usually, me and my Wolf's side lived amicably together, but now we both wanted different things.

I stationed an additional guard in the basement and immediately shifted to run through the woods. A pleasant run was usually enough to get both sides of me in agreement again, but even now, my wolf kept growling stupid things. *Mate, mine, mark him, take him.*

I had to shut it out or I would march back into that basement and do exactly that. Why couldn't I do that? No, we needed information, and I needed to keep my Pack safe.

"What do we know of the Vamp?" I asked my Beta through our Pack link.

He immediately responded, giving me the little information they had extracted from him. His name was, Elijah. It suited him, rolling easily off my tongue. Besides that, he only told my pack that he was just passing through and had missed the border signs. Which was of course impossible. Our borders were impregnated with Pack magic so no one could pass them without actively wanting to. It helped keep humans and unintelligent creatures out.

We needed more info, and I felt like I should be able to get it out of him. After my run and a quick shower, I went back to the basement. Dismissing my guards again, I entered the room.

"So Elijah, ready to cooperate?"

His head shot up, he looked even worse than when I left. His chains looked tightened, digging into his flesh. The little blood he had taken from me, must have already left his system, his healing not able to catch up with his wounds.

"As I told your minions, I am just passing through."

His voice was ragged. He coughed and some black substance leaked from the corner of his mouth. This was no way to get information out of him. I put on the gloves and loosened his chains so they didn't dig into his skin as hard. Getting rid of the unnecessary ones, I could already see his body working to heal. He would need blood I knew. Without the necessary substance, his body would attack itself trying to heal the wounds. Throwing the gloves aside I stepped in front of him. After a moment of hesitation, I cut my wrist with one of my sharp nails. I held it in front of his mouth. He eyed me warily.

"Is this another of your tricks? I am tired of your games, Wolf."

I pushed my wrist to his lips, silencing him. With a flick of his tongue, he lapped up my blood. When he tasted me, he moaned loudly, licking up more and more. That utter, sexual, male sound vibrated through me, making my body fire up. Waves of pleasure radiated through me, and he had only touched my wrist. The act of letting him drink my blood was so extremely erotic that I could have climaxed from just that. Without realizing I had come closer and crawled on his lap again. I rubbed myself all over him like a horny dog, while he licked and sucked up my blood.

Mate, vibrated through my head again. It was hard to keep denying it when the signs were all there. But I couldn't mark him yet. First, I needed my information.

Before it could go too far, I pulled my arm back. A low malicious growl sounded from him and I smiled. I had him right where I wanted to. The fact that he was hardening between my legs, and rubbed me just deliciously had nothing to do with it. I ground myself on him, looking at his reaction.

"If you want another taste, you tell me why you are in my territory," I said and waved my bleeding wrist in front of him.

His nostrils flared, his eyes darkened, and he made that delectable sound again. A drop of my blood threatened to fall down, so I held my wrist up high. It fell in my waiting mouth. He moaned loudly when I licked my lips, the coppery taste of my blood exploding in my mouth.

"Just passing through," he said between gritted teeth.

Another drop threatened to fall. I wasn't quick enough to catch it with my tongue. It fell down between my breasts. A strangled moan came from his throat when he saw the drop slide down lower until it disappeared from view.

"What a waste," I said, dipping my finger in my cleavage, retrieving the drop, and licking it up.

My healing kicked in, and no more drops escaped, but the streaks still painted my wrist and underarm red. The room smelled of my blood, mixed with my arousal, and his unique scent.

I waved my arm in front of him again. His jaws tightened, his breathing accelerated and his red eyes darkened.

"Ready to start talking?" I asked.

I put one of my sharp fingernails on his throat, cutting him just lightly.

"It would be a shame to have to kill you."

That earned me a choked laugh.

"You can kill me, about as much as I can resist you."

I looked at him with my head cocked to the side. A small smile grazed my lips.

"So you admit to being attracted to me?"

"Not much point in denying it," he said, nodding at his erection, hard, rubbing me between my legs.

"Maybe we should just fuck and get it over with," I said, trying to sound casual but failing miserably with my breathless voice.

He licked his hips, his eyes focused on my throat. "Maybe we should."

We looked at each other for a tantalizing second, but then I broke the spell. I picked up the glove and the silver.

"But first, you need to tell me why you are passing through my territory."

A strangled laugh escaped him. "Ironically, I did it to be faster. I have a message for my Queen that is important, but by now it will have no value left."

A message for the Vampire Queen? That could be very valuable in the hands of my pack. If it truly had a time frame to be delivered, it must have been very important.

"Poor Vampire. Caught in the clutches of a Wolf." I leaned forward, licking the shell of his ear. "You must know that I will never let you out of my sight again. You're mine now."

Choked sounds escaped him. My words flowed naturally and felt right. I hadn't expected it, but somehow the Moon Goddess had chosen this one for me. Now it was time to seal our bond, make him mine, and then see what to do about that message to the Vampire Queen. I got rid of the silver chains around him, except for his cuffs.

"What makes you think you can keep me?" he asked between gritted teeth.

I smiled at him. "The Moon Goddess has decided."

He sputtered. "You think I am your Mate? That is ridiculous!"

Taking a step closer, I leaned over him. "Have you ever felt like this? Like you wanna rip my clothes off, and fuck me until the sun comes up?"

He narrowed his eyes. "That is just some spell you let a Witch put on me."

I shook my head, my hair falling around my face, enveloping us both. "No spell, just the mating bond. I'll prove it to you."

I loosened his cuffs, freeing him of the last of his chains, and stepped back, arms wide. I gestured at the door. "You're free to go if you want, but I know that your instincts will tell you to come back and Mate me."

In a flash, he stood by the door grinning. "Foolish wolf."

A moment later he was gone. I stood there still with my arms wide, a smile on my face. It wouldn't take long. The Wolf inside of me was screaming to chase him, but I knew he had to come back to me, willingly.

A low growl sounded in the basement, and suddenly he stood before me again.

"One fuck, and then I am out of here," he said and attacked my mouth.

We stumbled around the basement, groping each other. Clothes were thrown around, and hot and cold naked skin met each other. His cool body felt delicious against mine.

"I want to taste you again," he said, licking the side of my neck.

A full-body shudder went through me. I wanted him to taste me as well. And I wanted to taste him. I needed to stake my claim and mark him as mine for everyone to see. But I had to wait, I couldn't claim him now, or I would scare him off. The best mating bonds were forged during the height of pleasure, so I would have to resist my urge to bite and savor him now.

"Do it," I said.

Immediately he latched on. His teeth pierced my skin, and he started sucking. Ripples of pleasure vibrated through me. My core clenched, and I could feel wetness seeping out. I was so ready for him to fuck me, but his bite did things to me I had never experienced.

Far too quickly he let off. Before I could protest, his head dived lower to my breasts. A gasp escaped me when he bit me just above my nipple. It was such a sensitive spot. My nipples hardened, and sounds of pleasure escaped me. I grasped his head, holding him at my chest, caressing his hair. He switched breasts, and more pleasure flowed through me. I never thought that getting bit could be so erotic.

When he had his fill on that area, he knelt before me, pushing me into the chair. My naked ass felt cold on the unwavering metal. He grasped my legs, opened me wide, and growled hungrily when the scent of my arousal greeted him. He kissed his way up one leg, pausing at the junction of my thigh and hip. I made a throaty sound of need. Looking me in the eye, he flicked out his tongue, marking the area. His penetrating gaze only heightened my arousal when he bit me there. The sensation shot straight through my pussy, and I moaned loudly, having to hold on to the chair to not lose my balance.

With a mouth covered in my blood, he grinned at me and licked his lips. I mimicked the movement, and he groaned. He dove again, giving my pussy a hard lick, before going to my other leg. Following the same path, he arrived at that sensitive spot. Another flick of his tongue, before he bit me again. I let my head fall back, reveling in the sensation of it.

He started sucking, switching location every once in a while. My blood and my juices covered his mouth, and it was the most erotic sight ever. The pleasure inside of me kept growing and growing with each flick of his tongue.

My healing kicked in, and the wounds on my legs closed. This made him focus solely on my pussy. He licked, nibbled, and sucked on my clit, making me gasp with pleasure. I could feel my climax fast approaching. I just needed something to push me over the edge.

A graze of one of his fangs over my sensitive clit was enough. He didn't bite me, but he did knick me, giving me a delicious burn. He sucked up the drop of blood together with the release of my orgasm. Waves of pleasure washed over me, as he kept sucking on my clit. My body trembled with my release. Pain mixed with pleasure was the most delicious feeling in the world, and me and my Wolf loved it.

As soon as my body stopped shaking, I jumped up and tackled him. With an oomph, he hit the ground, and I was on top of him.

"Mine," I growled before I could stop myself.

His eyes narrowed, and in the blink of an eye, he had turned us around so I was on the cold hard ground.

"Not yet," he said, hanging over me.

He hadn't denied my claim, simply evaded it for the time being. Then I must show him he is mine. We turned over again, and before he could react, I had shackled one of his arms with the silver. My hand burned from where I touched it, but my healing quickly took over.

I looked at his impressive erection and licked my lips. I wanted to devour him whole, but if I didn't feel him inside of me and complete our mating bond, I think my Wolf would take over.

"Pretty big for a vamp," I whispered.

Before he could give me a smart retort, I straddled him. Gripping his erection, I let myself slink over him slowly. He filled me perfectly, stretching me to just the edge of my comfort zone. Our growls of pleasure filled the basement.

"Pretty tight for a Wolf," he gasped.

I leaned over, moving so he slid out of me. My pussy contracted to try to keep him inside of me.

"Your first, and your last," I said against his lips.

Our kiss was filled with passion and something more. It was too early to speak of love, but the mating bond vibrated between us. There was no denying it.

Breaking off the kiss, I moved, so he slid inside of me again. His hungry growls mixed with my pleasurable moans filled the basement. I rode him at a quick and punishing pace. I needed another release, and I needed to mark him as mine.

He used his free hand, to slip between us, and stroke my clit. My muscles tightened around him. It wouldn't be long before my climax would take over. I leaned over again, while still moving my hips in a pleasurable rhythm. He met me thrust for thrust.

"Mine," I said again, and this time he didn't reply.

He just looked at me, and I could see so many emotions in his eyes. Anger, fear, longing, but also a tinge of something strong, but not yet love.

I slowly went for his neck, giving him every opportunity to stop me. He only sighed. A sound so lonely and lost that I could feel my heart clench. After this, neither of us should ever feel alone again. We would be one, always together, always by each other's side. I didn't know how we would navigate our two worlds, but we would make it work. The Moon Goddess had decided it.

Sniffing his neck, I savored his scent. Soon mine would be mixed in so everyone would know, who he belonged to, with just one sniff. I licked his velvety soft skin, reveling in his taste. I marked out the spot I would make mine with my tongue. A soft moan escaped him with every flick of my tongue.

My complete focus was on his neck, so he took over our lovemaking. His hips pumped up, and he kept thrusting inside of me while stroking my clit. My climax came closer with each movement he made. After another flick of my tongue, I could feel him tremble beneath me. He was as close as me. As soon as my teeth would connect to his skin, we would both shatter.

Soft, hungry noises escaped me, while I nuzzled his neck once more. I wanted to savor this moment, to be able to come back to it and cherish our Mating. My muscles started to contract around him, the build-up inside of me threatening to break, and I knew the moment was there.

After another sweep of my tongue, I pierced his skin with my teeth. I bit down hard, marking his hard skin with my bite. The taste of his blood exploded in my mouth. The mating bond snapped into place, and I could feel my orgasm take over my body. Pleasure like I never felt before washed over me. My whole body trembled and my muscles squeezed around him. A hoarse cry left him when he came with me.

His mouth latched on my shoulder and he bit me too. More pleasure flowed, and I could feel his pleasure as well. Our Mating bond was strong and sparked between us. Our climaxes merged, grew, and felt like they would never end.

When we reached the peak together, our bodies slummed over each other, and our teeth left each other. With satisfaction, I could see my perfect mating mark on his neck, for everyone to see.

"Mine now and forever," I mumbled.

The End

Seducing the Orc

I love Dungeons and Dragons. So it sucked when I had to leave my D&D group because I couldn't stand to be in the same room as my ex. I have always gone for the nerdy quiet type of guys since I have more in common with them than with sports guys.

Luckily I found a new party quickly. Playing with different people was always exciting. You never knew if you would match up and if play styles would merge or collide.

I was toying with the hem of my favorite lucky shirt when the door opened, and my breath caught. Standing before me was a magnificent Orc. His dark green skin and his impressive build made something inside of me spark. A zing of pleasure shot through me, and I could feel moisture starting to seep out into my panties. I had never reacted to someone so strongly at a first-time meeting, but I knew he was mine somehow.

His dark eyes widened in surprise, and a low grumble resounded from his chest. That sound made something flutter inside of me. He was massive, looming over me, but I didn't feel afraid, I only felt aroused.

"Hi," I said breathlessly.

He opened his mouth, but no words came out, just a grunt that I could feel vibrating through me.

"Let the human in Gunnar, so we can start the campaign," someone shouted from behind him.

So Gunnar was his name. I liked it. As if a spell was broken, he suddenly shook his head. He ushered me inside, introducing me to the rest of the group.

"Everyone, this is our newest member, Mia. Mia, this is everyone."

When he said my name, a zing of pleasure coursed through me, leaving me breathless, awaiting his next words. He sat down on his end of the table, and I awkwardly waved to the rest of the group.

"Cool shirt," one of the Nagas said.

Looking down, I saw the big Slytherin snake on my shirt. It was my favorite shirt, and I thought it would help break the tension that might be with letting a woman join their Dungeons & Dragons group.

"Thank you, green is my favorite color," I said and my eyes shot to Gunnar, drinking in his green appearance.

He ignored my existence, focusing on something on the paper before him. A stab of disappointment shot through me, but I didn't let that deter me. I was here to play Dungeons & Dragons, and I was going to enjoy myself.

The group existed of me; a human, two Vampires, a Naga, and my Orc as Dungeon Master. I had only played in full human groups, so far, so it was fun to see how everyone played different characters. Gunnar, the DM was sitting next to me, and every time he said something with his deep rumbling voice, I could feel a spark of pleasure wash over me. I had never reacted to someone like this, and it was getting harder and harder to focus on the game.

My cousin had mated to a Wolfman a few weeks back, and she had described the experience to me as feeling as if all the pieces of the puzzle suddenly fit when you met him. Could Gunnar be my Mate? I didn't know that much about Orcs, so it could be.

Sitting beside me, I could feel his strong thigh against my knee. Every time he moved, his leg rubbed against me, and I could feel a shiver go through my body. I sneaked a look at his face and I wondered how his tusks would feel against my lips. His mouth was wider than mine, so how would that work? Would his tongue be bigger as well? Another shiver passed through my body, imagining his enormous tongue between my legs. I could feel my pussy clench, and wetness starting to gather.

"Sophia, Sophia. Hey Mia!"

An annoyed voice took me out of my daydream. I hadn't responded to my character names, so the Naga had retorted by using my real name.

"Sorry, yes I was..." Imagining our DM licking me and making me his. I could hardly say that, so I just focused on the game. "My turn?" I asked.

"Yes," Gunnar said in his sweet, deep voice. "There are three enemies. Two have already attacked."

I nodded, smiling gratefully at him. "Okay, I use my Hunters Snare on that one. I ready my arrow and shoot at the hand holding his sword," I said. Rolling my die I asked, "Does an 18 hit?"

"Yes," Gunnar answered, and I had to restrain myself to not moan at his husky tone.

I rolled my other dies, counted up the damage, and passed my turn. It was hard keeping my attention on the game when everything Gunnar said made me squirm and wanted me to beg him to fuck me. The rest of the evening passed pleasantly, and we defeated the Dragon together as a team.

When everyone finally left, I stayed behind to help clean up. Putting the bowls away in the kitchen, I hummed to myself. When I turned around, Gunnar stood behind me. For such an enormous monster, he moved as quietly as a mouse.

I smiled up at him, straining my neck to look at him.

"Thank you for letting me join your campaign."

"No problem," Gunnar said.

The look in his eyes made my confidence return. He might have ignored me all evening, but the lust radiating from him was enough to feed my flame of mine as well. I took a step forward, and he backed up. Taking another, and another step, I cornered him against his kitchen cabinets.

"A big Orc like you, surely isn't afraid of a tiny human like me?" I asked, batting my lashes at him.

He swallowed audibly.

"No... No, I was just..."

"Do you feel it as well?" I asked, raising my hand to gently caress his muscular chest.

I had been getting aroused all evening. With every one of his words and movements, even when he just breathed.

"Doesn't your kind believe in Mates?" I asked.

"Yes... We do, but..."

"I never expected to get a Mate," I mussed, caressing lower and lower to the edge of his pants.

The sturdy fabric was straining to contain all of him. It seemed that I hadn't been alone in my arousal.

"Did you?"

"Huh?"

Gunnar seemed as distracted with my ministrations as I was getting. I could feel my arousal flood my panties and craved to get him inside of me.

"Did you expect to find a Mate tonight?"

"No, no, I never."

He sounded so strained that I took a step back, not touching him anymore.

"Are you disappointed that I am human? Would you reject me?"

"What? No!" he growled out.

Taking as much encouragement as I could, I stepped closer to him. Grabbing his pants, I quickly undid his button and zipper. His protest was smothered when I grabbed his massive cock in my hands. I couldn't encompass him. Not even both my hands could fit around him.

"I... I don't think this will fit," I whispered in awe of his cock.

It was massive, hard, and a shade darker green than the rest of him. The veins running along his length were almost black and angry looking.

"It will."

I looked up and saw his cheeks turn a darker green shade. Was my nerdy Orc blushing?

"How?" I asked, curious to see what he would say.

I had read some things about Orc's, but most of my information came from smutty romance novels, so I didn't know how accurate that information was.

"My... my seed will..." Gunnar stuttered. After a deep breath, he continued. "My seed will help."

I cocked my head, amused by the embarrassment showing on his face.

"So your seed will help me take your massive cock inside of me?" I asked, my voice taking on a breathless tone.

The green on his cheeks darkened even more, and I chuckled. I had a mate, a sexy, shy, nerdy one. I couldn't have picked out a better one for myself. We would get to know each other for the rest of our lives together. I would never have to date again. Having the security of our mating connection was almost enough to make me come right there in his kitchen. Excitement coursed through me.

"Maybe I should taste it then?" I asked, leaning forward.

He was so tall that I didn't even have to get on my knees to be able to take him in my mouth. A slight bend in my back was enough to make my mouth level with his cock. With a tentative sweep of my tongue, I tasted him. His aroma was nothing I could have prepared for. He didn't taste like pistachios, as I had read in a romance novel once. Gunnar tasted like the way fresh moss smelled, a green, earthy kind of aroma very uniquely him. His flavor exploded in my mouth, and I moaned in delight.

A low growl sounded above my head. Looking up, I could see my Orc with his eyes closed and face contorted in pleasure. I felt powerful. One sweep of my tongue had made this Orc tremble in desire, and he was all mine to do with as I pleased.

I opened my mouth to try to fit his head in. Even with my jaws as wide as I could, I only just fit in the tip. My teeth scrapped the sides, but he didn't seem to mind. Another guttural sound vibrated through the small kitchen. My delicious Orc Mate was quite vocal in his pleasure.

I used both of my hands to grip his impressive length. His cock was throbbing with his impending release. As I tried to suck on his head as hard as I could, I stroked his length with my hands. Gripping him tightly, I pushed my hands up and down, feeling all of him.

It didn't take long before his growls became louder and his hips started to thrust. I could feel his cock pulse in my hands. His cock expanded, almost choking me, and then his release filled my mouth. It was too much for me to swallow. His seed dripped from my lips as my throat worked to try to drink all of him down. My hands were covered, some was dripping down my chin to the kitchen floor, and even more, came out. The amount of seed he produced was absolutely mind-blowing. I could feel my muscles contract around emptiness, wondering how it would feel inside of me.

As soon as he finished coming, he picked me up and went straight for his bedroom. He let me fall down on the bed, and I giggled as I bounced on top of it. It was twice as wide as my king-size bed, big enough to fit a giant Orc. Gunnar growled and grabbed the hem of my shirt, ready to rip it into pieces.

"Don't you dare," I screamed, swatting away his big green hands. "This is my favorite shirt, and I will not let you destroy it."

This seemed to take him out of his aroused trance. He shook his head, and another cute blush appeared on his cheeks. I loved making him blush, and seeing him stare at me dazed, with his cock hanging out of his pants, made me giggle again. I didn't want to push my luck, so I quickly discarded my clothes, throwing them off the side of the bed. It was quite a high bed, his hips coming level with the mattress.

I opened my legs, giving him a good view of my wet pussy. He stepped closer, leaning over, and after a sniff, he growled low.

"Delicious."

Gunnar put his massive hand between my legs and swiped a finger between my pussy lips. His massive finger was almost as big as some of my exes' cocks. He pushed it inside and snarled a low, animalistic sound.

"So tight."

Warmth rushed to my cheeks at his statement. I was an average-sized woman, but next to him I looked petite.

"You will need more of my cum to make me fit," he said, straightening up again.

He grabbed his cock, still shiny with my saliva and some of his seed, and started to pull at it. The sight of him masturbating in front of me made me squirm on the bed. I let my hand slip between my legs, stroking my pussy in the same rhythm as he was doing.

"Come with me," Gunnar growled. "So you are nice and relaxed, ready for my fat Orc cock."

The shy Orc seemed to have disappeared with the blow job I had given him in his kitchen. Before me stood an Orc ready to claim his Mate and I loved it.

My legs started to tremble, and shivers of pleasure coursed through me as I could feel my muscles starting to clench around my fingers. I used my thumb to strum my clit, as I pushed in three fingers, chasing the same high as he.

His pace increased, and I could see his strong muscles standing out against his arm. His green skin gleamed with perspiration in the low light of his bedroom. He looked absolutely magnificent, grunting and stroking his delicious cock for me.

"Coming," Gunnar groaned as an only warning before he started to spray me with his seed.

His cum coated my belly and thighs. Even after having it in my mouth, and swallowing a lot of him, it still amazed me how much he could cum. After another grunt, he released the last spurt of his seed on me. His scent filled the bedroom and I felt like I was in a forest somewhere eons ago. A small human female, ready to be ravished by the massive Orc.

His hands were sticky with his release, and he leaned over me. Slowly he pushed one of his cum covered fingers inside of me, and I moaned, feeling him stretch me with only his finger. That feeling was enough to finally push me over the edge of my climax. Slight tremors racked my body from my orgasm, and his finger only added to my pleasure.

"So tight," he murmured.

After a few shallow thrusts, I could feel myself accommodating to his girth, and the pleasure started to build. His finger left my body, and a low, needy moan escaped me.

"Don't worry, my mate," Gunnar growled.

He dipped his fingers in the cum covering me and put it inside of me again.

"I'm going to make sure you're ready for my cock," he said, his voice low and husky.

It felt amazing, and when he added another finger, I could feel how his cum was helping me adapt to his size. He filled me with more and more of it until I could easily take three of his fingers. I still felt a small burn, but it was pleasurable, not painful.

"Please, I need you," I moaned.

I felt slippery and wet down there, and I knew I could take him now. His cum combined with my juices should be enough to make his entrance easy enough.

"I will mate you now," Gunnar rumbled.

"Yes, mate me, fuck me, breed me, make me yours forever," I moaned.

He pulled my hips closer to the edge until my butt balanced on the side. Stepping between my legs, he loomed over me, and again I was amazed at how this wonderful Orc was my mate. His eyes searched mine, and when he saw the determination and lust in them, he grabbed his cock to place between us.

It looked massive between my legs, and a slight tinge of worry entered my mind. Would it fit?

Gunnar erased that worry from my mind as soon as he started to push in. Very slowly and gently, he entered me. I could feel a low burn fill me but combined with the amazing feeling of being stretched and filled to the brim, pleasure sparked. Inch after delicious inch entered me, and it felt like he was meant to be there all along.

"Fuck you're tight," Gunnar growled as he slid further inside of me.

Sounds of pleasure left my mouth that I had never heard produce before. He was doing things to me that I didn't even know were possible. As soon as he bottomed out, both of us emitted sounds, calling out our pleasure.

"Perfect fit," Gunnar mumbled, looking in awe at the place we were joined.

I tilted up my hips to try to make him move, but there was no way I could budge this massive Orc.

"Please Gunnar. I need you to fuck me," I begged.

My words spurred him on, and he began to move. Slowly he pulled out until only his thick head was inside of me to then plunge back deep. Each thrust touched nerve endings that have never been touched before. The pleasure inside of me was rising, shivers coursed through my body, and I could feel myself tightening around him. I just needed something more to be able to come.

I let one hand slip between us, stroking my clit, enhancing my pleasure. His eyes focused on my movements, and he followed them, almost entranced. Gunnar kept a steady pace. While my climax grew with each thrust of his cock and flick on my clit. Another growl from him vibrated through me and ignited my orgasm. I let out a shout of pleasure and I could feel it consume me. Waves of pleasure washed over me, and my muscles tightened around him. He growled again, thrusting into me harder, prolonging my climax.

My brain was filled with endorphins, but I could see he was holding himself back somehow.

"Take me how you want, my mate," I mumbled, satisfied with my second orgasm of the night.

His cheeks darkened again, and amusement filled me. My sweet, shy, nerdy Orc, perfect for me.

"Tell me what you want," I said, my voice hoarse from the screams of pleasure.

"I... I want to... try..." he closed his mouth and shook his head, pulling out of me. "It is not okay to ask, you wouldn't..."

I grabbed his cock, efficiently cutting off his words. I pulled him back, not wanting to lose our connection yet.

"Don't tell me what I don't want. What do you want to try?"

Gunnar took a deep breath and his eyes shot everywhere but at my face. I squeezed his hard cock, and a gasp left him.

He closed his eyes, and after another deep breath said, "I want to fuck you on my cock like a rag doll."

My breathing hitched, and my muscles clenched around him. That was the sexiest thing anyone had ever said to me. I appreciated his honesty and was more than a bit turned on by his proposition.

"Yes," I said, and his eyes shot up to my face.

The eagerness in them made my muscles clench around his cock again, earning me another growl from him. I opened my mouth to say something but quickly lost whatever thought was in my mind when he grabbed me. In a swift move uncharacteristic of such a big Orc, he had us switched around. He sat on the edge of the bed, and he had me positioned on top of his cock.

He looked at me with searching eyes, but after an encouraging nod from me, he pulled me down on top of him, spearing me on his cock. This time, he wasn't gentle. Gunnar used me like a fuck toy specifically made for him. My whole body felt limp with pleasure. I pushed out my hands, grazing his chest to keep me from toppling over when he rutted into me like an animal. Hard and fast strokes made me feel used in the best way.

The small bedroom was filled with the sounds of the slapping of meat, my breathy moans, and his unrestrained, guttural groans. I looked at his face, and his look of ecstasy made me even hotter. He looked feral, ready to lose control, like the monster he was on the outside. I knew he was the perfect, shy, nerdy Orc mate for me on the inside, but I loved this animalistic side that came out in the bedroom.

"Fuck, you feel amazing Mia," Gunnar growled while he pulled me down on his massive cock again and again.

"You too," I moan, and by magic, I could feel another orgasm starting to rise inside of me.

I was starting to lose count of the number of times either of us had come already. His growls grew deeper, and I could feel his cock starting to expand inside of me, signaling his impending release. I wanted to join him, so I let my hand slip down to caress my clit. Looking down at the place where we were joined, I moaned. His massive cock was pummeling inside of me, and my pussy was stretched around him obscenely. The amount of fluid between us was almost ridiculous. My wetness mixed with his seed looked filthy and perfect at the same time.

Another deep growl sounded from him, and while I watched, his cock expanded. I could feel and see it spasm and throb as he came deep inside of me.

He filled me to the brink, and some leaked out at all sides. His cock, now covered with his seed, kept sliding in and out of me. His climax triggered my own, and I could feel the waves of pleasure wash over me. My pussy clenched around him, milking him for all he was worth.

He pulled me down one last time, burring deep inside of me so his seed would stay put. His arms came around me, and he hugged me close to his chest. His hands fluttered, caressing me gently while his mouth was buried in my hair.

"Thank you, thank you," Gunnar repeated in a muffled voice.

"What for?" I asked in a hoarse voice.

He looked at my face, and the emotions in his eyes almost made me choke up.

"For letting me do this to you, for trusting me, for being my mate, for everything," Gunnar said.

With the last of my strength, I raised my hand and cupped his cheek. My thumb caressed his tusk, and I smiled.

"Yours forever, mate."

The End

Bonus Story: On a Date with the Naga

So I was on a date with a Naga. The same Naga I let fuck my asshole and pussy at the same time. I would probably get fired for that, but it had been too good to regret.

Right after our little encounter at the library, I had demanded we went out for a coffee. I needed time to figure out how to handle the situation, and I didn't want him to report me without having a grasp on what had happened.

It felt a bit awkward to sit across from a creature that knew me more intimately than others, but not even knowing his name. I gasped, feeling like a slut.

His eyes shot up from his coffee and focused on me.

"What?" he asked, with his delicious voice.

It felt like silk flowing over me. I wanted to hear him speak more. I wished he would say all kinds of dirty stuff while fucking me again. Gods, there was definitely something wrong with me.

"We haven't even exchanged names, but we have... you know."

He smiled, showing me his pointy teeth.

"I know your name. You have been the auditor for our library for as long as I have worked there."

"You do?" I asked.

"Avery," he said, focusing slightly on the last letter as his tongue slithered out. "I have watched you every time you came in, hoping you would give me some of your attention. Always a dream until today. I am Ezra."

"Ezra," I repeated, trying out his name on my tongue.

I couldn't form the Z as well as he could, but I liked it. His eyes were focused on my mouth and he moaned softly when I said his name.

"I love my name on your lips," he said.

My breath caught. "So you're not gonna report me to my superior?"

"Report you? You have made all my dreams come true. I would want to thank him."

I smiled and leaned over closer to him. "All your dreams?"

He blushed, his green scales turning a shade darker. "Maybe not all."

"Tell me about them."

I started to get turned on, talking to this Naga, no talking to Ezra in the coffee shop across from the library. We really shouldn't be doing this, but boy did I want to.

One of his tongues flitted out, tasting the air. He probably knew how turned on I was getting just by having this conversation. His scales darkened again, giving him a beautiful dark green color. I was fascinated by his scales, the color, the way they had felt against my back when he fucked me... And my mind had turned dirty again.

He leaned closer. My eyes focused in on his mouth. How would it feel against mine? He had almost no lips, but his tongues must feel heavenly.

"I have always wanted to try something," he said.

His tone was husky. I leaned in as well, catching his delectable scent, my muscles clenched around nothing. My panties started to get wet, and I wanted to feel his cocks inside of me again.

"What?" I asked, my voice a breathless whisper in the bustling of the coffee shop.

His tongue slid out again, wetting his thin lips. Ezra swallowed and said, "Stuffing someone with both my cocks at the same time."

"But we did..." My voice broke off when understanding dawned.

My eyes widened, and my insides clenched again. He wanted to stuff my pussy with both his cocks. I swallowed, my throat suddenly parched.

It seemed like his confidence vanished when I didn't have any reply to his confession. My mind was whirling, envisioning all kinds of scenarios and visions of how that would fit and feel inside of me. He pulled back, scales dark green, his eyes darted around the coffee shop as if to find an exit.

I grabbed his hand before he could get up, the scales hard beneath my fingers. Ezra froze, eyes on me. I licked my lips, slow and deliberate.

"What if..." I said, taking a moment to elongate the tension. "I would want you to do to that to me right now."

His breath came out in a huff. He closed his eyes for a moment. When he opened them again, I could see the fire of passion burn hot.

"What if I said that my apartment is just down the street?" Ezra said.

I smiled, leaning closer, caressing his jaw with my fingers. His scales felt cool beneath my touch. He closed his eyes, reveling in it.

"Then I would say, let's get the check and get to your apartment."

WE STUMBLED INTO HIS bedroom, tearing each other's clothes off. Before I knew it, I was naked on his bed, spread wide.

He leaned in between my legs, both his tongues flicking out, tasting the air. Finally, I could look at him in all his glory. His scales shifted in color from dark to light green, creating a beautiful pattern over his chest, and lower to his twin cocks, almost as if to mark the way. Both his cocks were hard and dripping with precum. I had them inside of me already, but suddenly my throat felt dry at the thought of both of them stuffing my pussy full.

My pussy clenched as if she agreed with the proposition. Wetness seeped out, and Ezra's eyes focus on it. Like the predator he was, he slowly inched closer. I had nowhere to run, and I didn't want to. I needed to feel his cocks inside of me; I needed him to fill me up like no one had ever done before.

He opened his mouth, and I saw both his tongues slither out at the same time. They were long, thick, and wet. Ready to prep me to be able to take him. I was producing a lot of wetness already, but for this endeavor, we needed more. He licked me, and I moaned. Both his tongues were working me in a way that make my toes curl. But I needed his cocks.

"Fuck me," I moaned.

He slithered higher, leaning over me, caging me in with his big form.

"Do you need my cocks?" Ezra said, his eyes focused on me with a piercing gaze.

The shy Naga from before had disappeared, and before me stood a male who knew exactly what he wanted and how to get it, and I loved it. I had enjoyed commanding him in the library, but this was even better. He was going to take me for his own pleasure, and I wanted it all.

"Yes, I need you to fuck me. Fill me up with both of them."

He hissed menacingly. A shiver went down my spine. I didn't know if it was from fright or excitement. He grabbed his upper cock and placed it at my entrance. Very slowly, he slid inside of me. I could take him easily. His size was pleasurable, but not too big. Little bursts of pleasure flashed through my body with each thrust. The ridges on his cock made every movement feel amazing. He thrust into me a few times, just enough to make me want more. I was moaning and moving around to bed, trying to find the right friction to give me more pleasure.

Just when I thought I had found a spot, he pulled out and positioned his lower cock at my pussy. He pushed in, and I reveled in the same but different feeling. There was something different between his two cocks, but I couldn't pinpoint what. My thoughts disappeared when he started fucking me again. My muscles squeezed around him, and the pleasure that had started building grew bigger.

When I begged for more, he pulled out. Both his cocks were shiny with my juices. He spit in his hands, to lubricate even more, and I moaned at the sight of him fondling himself. His eyes focused on me when I made that sound. He leaned over to lick at my pussy again. Using his fingers he spread me wide and admired my pussy.

"So tight," Ezra hissed, almost to himself. "But I will make it fit."

He grabbed both his cocks with his one hand and opened my pussy lips with the other. He positioned himself at my entrance and pushed. I could feel my body try to accommodate, but it was too much. He was too much, he would tear me. I could feel myself stretch until it burned. It would never work. But suddenly a soft pop sounded, and both his cocks entered me. I was breathing heavily, moaning and begging at the same time. It was too much; it felt too good. I had never felt so full in my entire life.

"Yes, take it," he groaned, pushing deeper into me.

He had to push hard to fill me entirely. Words and sounds of pleasure left my mouth without my mind realizing it.

"Oh, yes Ezra," I moaned.

His whole body went ridged, and a growl sounded from him. My breathing caught. Had I done something wrong? The realization that he was a dangerous predator that could kill me in the blink of an eye came over me.

He leaned closer, his lips a breath away from mine.

"Say my name again," he said.

"Ezra," I whispered, not daring to speak too loud.

"Again," he moaned, and he started to move.

His thrusts were hard and focused, as if he wanted to drive me to the edge as fast as possible. Shivers of pleasure racked my body, and I had a hard time focusing on what he had said.

"Ezra, please," I moaned.

His name only spurred him on, so I kept on saying it, moaning it, begging it. His eyes turned feral and his pace quickened even more. He was fucking me so hard that the bed was scrapping across the floor. His hands on my hips were the only thing that kept me from shooting off the bed. Pleasure started to bubble up, the fire inside me stoked with his every movement.

I just needed a little something to push me over the edge, but my mind was too far gone to ask. My voice became hoarse from saying his name like a prayer. Something in my tone must have tipped me off, because suddenly his body moved. He slithered in a way that made his cocks sink even deeper inside of me. My mind became mush. Ezra pushed every pleasure point inside me, stroking every inch of me, but still.

Just then I could feel a pressure at my clit. My eyes shot down and I could see the end of his tail on my clit. It circled around it slowly, lazily, as if we had all the time in the world. The pressure inside of me built up, as he kept his thrusts hard and even.

A low hiss made my eyes shot up. His tongues slithered out, tasting the air.

"Come for me," Ezra said.

His tail focused on my clit, increasing the pressure, and I burst up in flames. Pleasurable waves crashed over me, and my whole body trembled and quaked. My muscles tightened around his cocks, making it hard for him to move. With a curse, he started to come as well. His twin cocks pulsed and sprayed me full with his seed.

He thrust a few more times before he pulled out. I could feel his cum gushing out, but his fingers stopped me. He collected his seed and pushed it inside of me again. I looked and moaned when I saw his tongues flit out again.

"Nice and full," Ezra murmured.

This had been the second time he had come inside of me, and I realized I loved it more and more. I might be falling for this Naga.

The End

Authors Note

So the Bonus story follows right after the Bonus story in my first collection. I felt like this couple hadn't met their ending yet and suddenly I had all of these ideas on how their relationship would progress one spicy scene at a time. So with every Creature Loving Collection you will get a bonus story featuring our lovely Ezra and Avery!

I hope you enjoy them because I have many more sexy ideas on how they will meet!

About the author

Lilith Leana writes what she loves; Monster erotica.

Born and raised in Belgium, she devours ebooks as if it heals her. In her day job she loves to organize, plan and make schedules for other people, but when the night falls she can let loose with her fantasies which star all kinds of Monsters and Human couplings.

YOU CAN ALSO FIND ME on:

Author Home Page: https://lilithleanaauthor.start.page/

Instagram: https://www.instagram.com/lilithleana/

Or you can email me: lilith.leana666@gmail.com

DEAR READER

If you enjoyed this book, please consider leaving a review. Indie writers depend on reviews to keep writing and publishing.

Thank you so much ❤

Lilith

Also by the author

Series & Collections

<u>Creature Loving Volume 1: A Monster Erotica Collection</u>[1]
My Ghostly Lover[2] - Full story: 3 Parts + Epilogue
Part I: Taken by the Ghost[3]
Part II: Freeing my Ghost[4]
Part III: Saving my Ghost[5]

Standalone Short Stories

<u>Sniffed by the Dragon</u>[6]
<u>Deal with the Demon</u>[7]
<u>Servicing the Minotaur</u>[8]
<u>Captured by the Wendigo</u>[9]
<u>Bathing with the Akkorokamui</u>[10]
<u>Courted by El Sombrerón</u>[11]
<u>Saved by the Yeti</u>[12]

---

1. https://books2read.com/u/47gLkj

2. https://books2read.com/u/3J6dxJ

3. https://books2read.com/u/3yVerv

4. https://books2read.com/u/mBvKok

5. https://books2read.com/u/bwrZN9

6. https://books2read.com/u/boy8vV

7. https://books2read.com/links/ubl/3kYPzN

8. https://books2read.com/u/md1P5w

9. https://books2read.com/u/b5jJAk

10. https://books2read.com/u/3LVqEX

11. https://books2read.com/u/38PLpB

<u>Mated to a Vampire</u>[13]
Seducing the Orc

Holiday Short Stories

<u>Helping the Green Goblin Steal Christmas</u>[14]

Coming Soon

Bedding the God of Dreams - 14 January
Saved by the Grim Reaper
The House of Desire: Multiple part Series - Coming Soon - 2023

12. https://books2read.com/u/bQj7VP

13. https://books2read.com/u/m2d8Y6

14. https://books2read.com/u/mZEGjR

Sneak Peak of my next story:
Bedding the God of Dreams

"*You dare defy a King in his own court? A God in his own world?*"

His booming voice sent shivers through my body. This was more than a mere dream, I realized too late. What I knew for certain about dreams was that you should never show your fear. I took a deep breath to calm my fluttering heart.

"I do," I said, bracing for his wrath.

A low, throaty chuckle resounded. It sounded rusty, like he hadn't used it in a long time. His stormy eyes lightened and I could see more stars twinkle in them.

"It has been a while since someone defied me," he said with a small quirk of his mouth.

I smiled back. "It has been a while since a dream got away from me." I bit my lip and leaned a bit closer. "Usually I call the shots in my dream."

"Do you now?" he said, not moving away. "I have seen all the dreams in my realm, but I don't think I have seen yours."

"I can show you if you want?"

"Would you be so kind?"

"More selfish than kind," I replied, focusing my eyes on his lips.

I hadn't gotten my usual release that I got from my dreams yet. His lips drew me in. Dreaming of desire and arousal was definitely not the same as experiencing it for real. I didn't know where I was, but it was somewhere between a dream and real life. It felt more real than any dream I had experienced so far, and I wanted to experience more of it with him.

His eyes shot to my lips as well. A low sound of need filled the empty space between us. I didn't know which one of us made it.

"It has been ages since I let myself indulge in the pleasures of the flesh," he said.

"Indulge in me, oh God of Dreams," I whispered.

Adding his title had the desired effect. He closed the gap between us, and his lips met mine. The kiss was everything I had ever dreamed of, and somehow at the same time, so much more. I moaned in his mouth, revelling in the all-encompassing taste of his lips. He tasted like all of my dreams, a swirl of my hopes and desires mixed into a delicious cocktail unique to my taste. Impossible to describe, but the most delicious sensation ever.

Bedding the God of Dreams – Coming Soon – 14 January

Don't miss out!

Visit the website below and you can sign up to receive emails whenever Lilith Leana publishes a new book. There's no charge and no obligation.

https://books2read.com/r/B-A-YTZU-EYBEC

BOOKS2READ

Connecting independent readers to independent writers.